RISE OF
THE REBELS

BASED ON STORIES BY GREG WEISMAN,
HENRY GILROY, AND SIMON KINBERG

WRITTEN BY MICHAEL KOGGE

D1333485

To all those new rebels, about to take
their first steps into a larger world.
—M.K.

EGMONT

We bring stories to life

First published in Great Britain 2014
by Egmont UK Limited, The Yellow Building,
1 Nicholas Road, London W11 4AN.

ISBN 978 1 4052 7580 4
59245/1
Printed in Italy

Stay safe online. Any website addresses listed in this book are correct at the
time of going to print. However, Egmont is not responsible for content hosted by
third parties. Please be aware that online content can be subject to change
and websites can contain content that is unsuitable for children.
We advise that all children are supervised
when using the internet.

CONTENTS

PART I
THE **MACHINE**
IN THE *GHOST*

CHAPTER 1
The Outer Rim.

It was the largest region of the known galaxy – and the loneliest. Much of it had not yet been mapped. Ships could travel the hyperlanes for years and never run into another soul.

Such was not the case for the *Ghost*. The sector of the Outer Rim where it travelled had suddenly become a very busy place. Four flat-winged Imperial TIE fighters screamed after the freighter in hot pursuit.

'Kanan.' Hera's voice crackled over the *Ghost*'s intercom. 'We have a small situation here.'

Kanan Jarrus hurried down the *Ghost*'s main corridor to the dorsal turret. He shook his head at Hera's words. *A small situation.* Hera loved to understate their challenges. It was her Twi'lek sense of humour.

In reality, there was nothing funny about being chased by TIEs. They were the Empire's fastest fighters, flown by the Empire's best pilots – pilots who were willing to surrender their lives for the greater glory of the New Order.

A TIE fighter's lasers shook the ship's shields, causing Kanan to bump into a wall. He grabbed the turret ladder to steady himself.

No. Their troubles were far bigger than just a *small* situation.

'And if you'd care to blast one of those TIEs out of the galaxy, I don't think anyone would object,' Hera said through intercom static.

'Working on it,' Kanan said, climbing the ladder into the turret. Internal microphones would transmit his voice back to Hera in the cockpit. 'But it's not like you gave me a lot of warning.'

'As I recall, raiding an Imperial convoy was your plan, love,' Hera said.

Kanan dropped into the turret's bucket seat. 'Well, it made sense at the time.'

And it had. They thought they had hit the jackpot when Chopper, their antique astromech droid, had unscrambled an Imperial military frequency. Comm chatter revealed that nearby cargo ships were transporting minerals used to build the Empire's war machines. But what Kanan and Hera hadn't known was that the Empire would have TIE fighters waiting for them. The cargo report had been a trap set to capture rebels.

Kanan didn't blame himself. He and Hera would've been lazy banthas if they hadn't done something about the transport convoy. Every chance to end the evil of the Empire had to be taken – no matter how great the risk. That was what Hera always said.

More lasers hammered the *Ghost*'s shields. A TIE roared over the freighter. Kanan grabbed the gun grips and spun in his seat, tracking the enemies.

The TIEs were indeed fast and hard to target. Yet speed had its sacrifices. The Empire had designed their fighters to be all engine, no shields. One or two direct hits could knock out a TIE for good.

The targeting computer beeped. It had a lock.

Kanan fired.

His shots nailed the TIE in one of its twin ion engines. The enemy pilot couldn't manoeuvre out of this. His craft exploded in a blaze of light.

Kanan whirled around in the turret. One down, three to go.

CHAPTER 2

Hera was nearly blinded

in the pilot's chair. First there was the explosion; then came a barrage of laser fire from the remaining TIEs. The light was so intense that even Hera's Twi'lek head-tails twitched.

Laser fire shouldn't be that bright. The shields should have lessened the intensity. It could mean only one thing.

'Shields down!' Hera shouted after checking her scopes. 'Chopper, fix them!'

Behind her, the astromech unit C1-10P, otherwise known as 'Chopper,' uttered a sound halfway between a snort and a beep. He was an old and moody little machine, always whining about this or that. But as much as the droid complained, and as out of date as his model was, Hera wanted no one else repairing the *Ghost*. Chopper connected with the ship's systems far better than any flesh-and-blood mechanic or new droid model ever could.

Chopper extended one of his repair arms into a socket and got to work. Meanwhile, Hera toggled switches on the control panel. They were going to need every boost of speed they had to avoid the TIEs until the shields were online again.

Kanan wasn't making their job any easier. His next shot completely missed. But the oncoming TIE didn't. Its lasers hammered the *Ghost*'s hull, rattling Hera in her seat.

She slapped the intercom. 'Kanan, what part of "blast them" did you not understand?' she said while steering the ship into an evasive roll.

Hera expected one of Kanan's wry replies.

HERA

He had a thousand one-liners ready to go. Humorous banter was their way of keeping their heads cool during life-and-death moments. But there was no response through the intercom.

'Kanan?' Hera stabbed at the intercom button again. 'Kanan, do you read?'

There was nothing but static. If the TIE's

blasts had somehow hit the turret and she'd lost Kanan, she didn't know what she'd do. Kanan Jarrus was more than a friend or a colleague. The human meant the world to her – although she'd never admit it to him.

A burst of cannon fire from the turret relieved her worries. Kanan was still there in the turret, fighting the good fight. The enemy's shot must have destroyed only a communication module.

'Internal comm is out,' Hera said to Chopper. 'Go back to comm control and fix it.'

Chopper let out a high-pitched whine that exasperated Hera. This was no time for complaining.

'I know you're fixing the shields,' Hera said, jerking the flight stick from side to side. 'But I need the comm operational to coordinate our attack. Now go before I pull your battery!'

Chopper grunted and withdrew his arm from the socket. A third round of cannon fire rang out from Kanan's turret. The closest TIE swerved around the bolts and came at the *Ghost* for another laser strafing run.

'And while you're back there,' Hera said as the droid rolled out of the cockpit, 'tell Kanan to please hit something!'

CHAPTER 3

Chopper trundled down the corridor, grumbling in low tones. *Do this, Chopper. Do that, Chopper.* Hera and Kanan were constantly telling him to get things done – things that always had to be done *now*. Yet when was the last time they had thanked him with a lubrication bath? It had been thirty-two days, twenty-three hours, fifty-seven minutes, and four seconds since his last dip. Parts of him were getting rusty. Rust slowed his joints.

Rust made his circuits misfire. Rust made him crabbier.

Chopper stopped before the turret. Inside, Kanan whirled in his seat, trying to get a lock on the approaching TIE.

Chopper chirped for Kanan to shoot better. The droid knew Kanan couldn't understand *exactly* what he said without a translation screen. That was one of the difficulties of working with organic beings. Their brains couldn't handle binary.

Kanan pressed the gun triggers. This round didn't miss. It reduced the enemy fighter to space dust.

'I'm a little busy, Chop,' Kanan said, scanning for the other two TIEs.

So am I, Chopper wanted to reply. But the droid kept those beeps to himself. He started to move away to the comm centre.

'Wait . . .' Kanan said. He looked down at the droid from the turret. 'What are you doing back here? Shouldn't you be fixing the shields?'

CHOPPER

Chopper rasped Hera's message to Kanan in binary.

Kanan shook his head and fired again. His shots kept the two TIEs from getting closer. 'Did you say you're fixing the comm?' he asked.

Chopper revolved his dome towards Kanan. The droid had to admit this human was one of the smarter organics he'd worked with. Kanan Jarrus often got the gist of what Chopper chirped.

Kanan didn't wait for Chopper's response as he pumped the cannons. 'Because I don't need to talk to "Captain" Hera right now. What I need is for you to get back there and fix the shields!'

Chopper groaned. He could have fixed either the shields or the comm unit during the 34.2 seconds he had wasted here. He turned around and headed back towards the cockpit.

'Oh, yeah,' Kanan yelled from the turret. 'When you see Hera, tell her to fly better.'

Chopper repeated his low-toned grumbles. Organics were so inefficient in communicating with each other.

Hera jerked the flight yoke right and left to avoid the TIEs' lasers. The navicomputer showed that the two fighters blocked the escape vector into hyperspace. If Kanan

couldn't do his job and blast them, she'd have to find a way to get rid of them.

Chopper re-entered the cockpit. The droid whistled something that sounded like she needed to fly better.

'Oh, he said that, did he?' Hera yanked the yoke to one side, pulling the *Ghost* in a fast arc around a TIE. Her fingers danced on the controls. The nose gun's targeting system came online. Almost immediately she had a lock on the TIE.

'Do I have to do everything myself?' she said, pressing the firing button.

The TIE stood no chance against her attack from behind. Its explosion reminded Hera of fireworks on her homeworld of Ryloth.

'There, I just reduced Kanan's targets by half.' Hera glanced past her green head-tails at the droid. 'Tell our fearless leader he should be able to handle one lone TIE fighter on his own.'

Chopper blurted out something and turned back toward the corridor.

'What was that?' Hera asked. She heard nothing more as the droid rolled off.

• • •

When Chopper was out of Hera's visual range, he angrily waved two of his repair arms back in her direction. This was ridiculous. Going back and forth, like a computer program caught in a never-ending loop. Meanwhile, without shields, the *Ghost* had nothing but a thin layer of hull plating to keep them all from being obliterated.

While Hera and Kanan might be reckless with their lives, Chopper actually cared about his circuits continuing to operate. And though he'd never tell them in binary, he cared about theirs, too. His programming instructed him to preserve their lives at all costs.

That was why he wheeled past the turret without stopping.

'Chopper?' Kanan said. The human must have heard the rust in his joints. 'Chopper, where are you going?'

Chopper didn't answer. There wasn't a microsecond to spare. His logic chips assured him that what he was doing wasn't disobedience, because Hera had not told Chopper precisely *when* to relay to Kanan what she'd said. Chopper could tell Kanan *after* he was finished saving them all.

REBEL GHOST

Chopper entered the *Phantom,* the small craft attached to the tail section of the *Ghost.* Its cockpit was cramped. Its control panel lacked multiple banks of switches and status gauges. It had no navicomputer, because it had no hyperdrive.

But the *Phantom* didn't need all those features. The vessel was designed for one function and one function only.

To fight.

Chopper extended his arm into the main socket. On the control panel, the targeting screen powered on. The droid uploaded a batch of commands.

Unlike the *Ghost,* which often responded rudely to what Chopper asked it to do, the *Phantom* followed Chopper's commands without objection. Its laser cannons angled towards the TIE fighter that streaked past. Chopper waited for the right moment to tell it to fire.

The Imperial pilot likely believed he had a

bull's-eye shot at the *Ghost*. But the pilot never got to unload his lasers. In the moment before he could fire, the *Phantom*'s cannons atomised the enemy ship.

Chopper headed back to the *Ghost*'s cockpit, this time tootling a victory tune.

'All right, I admit it,' Hera said from the cockpit. 'That was some fine shooting.'

Chopper rolled through the doorway and let out a string of triumphant beeps. Then he saw Kanan was also in the cockpit, facing Hera. 'Thanks. You too,' the human said to Hera.

Chopper realised that Hera hadn't been talking to him. Rather, the two organics were *communicating* with each other. And they were standing rather close to each other – a third of a metre closer than usual, to be exact.

Chopper excused himself with a sharp beep and moved to go.

'Just kidding, Chop,' Kanan said. He

turned away from Hera and crouched at the droid's level.

'We know you got the last one,' Hera said. 'Good work.'

Chopper looked at them for a moment, then waved away their praise with a socket arm. His circuits had trouble processing what organics wanted when they displayed too much emotion. It was illogical. It was what they called 'sappy'.

What Chopper wanted more than their praise was an oil bath. It had now been thirty-three days since –

'Now get that comm fixed,' Kanan said.

'And the shields. Don't forget the shields,' Hera said.

Chopper shifted his dome's photoreceptors from the human to the Twi'lek. Was this another display of emotion? Or one of their so-called jokes?

His logic chip couldn't figure out the

difference. But the chip did inform him that because his friends' lives were no longer in danger, he needed to attend to those duties they had requested.

As he went to do so, the droid popped off a long stream of grumbles.

'What was that?' Kanan and Hera asked.

Chopper rolled forward to a central computer socket. The *Ghost*'s complicated electronic systems and engines were things he could understand. Organics, on the other hand, tended to say one thing but mean something else.

And they obviously didn't understand the need for lubrication baths.

PART 2
ART **ATTACK**

CHAPTER 4

A thousand thousand worlds sparkled in the night sky above the capital city of Lothal.

Sabine found the view breathtaking as she scaled the city wall. The galaxy's Outer Rim was such a big place. So many planets, so many stars, with names like Lasan, Utapau, and Mandalore, her birth world. All teeming with mysteries and diverse species.

She wanted to visit them all. She wanted to have a thousand thousand adventures on those thousand thousand worlds. She wanted her name and her artwork to be known across the stars.

But that was impossible with the Empire in control of the galaxy.

The Imperials did everything they could to limit personal freedom, including suppressing creative talent. They cracked down on anyone whose work didn't glorify the Emperor's New Order.

Their efforts didn't frighten her in the least. They only made her want to paint more images that defied the Empire.

No one was going to squash Sabine Wren.

Hard *clack-clack*s echoed in the street below. Sabine recognised that sound immediately. Imperial stormtroopers.

She tightened her grip and leant close against the wall as she climbed. She must remain unseen. Stormtrooper blasters were hardly ever set to 'stun'.

She turned her head for a glance below. Her helmet's internal display magnified a squad of white-armoured stormtroopers surrounding some unlucky bystander. Their commander shoved the bystander to the ground.

'Move along! This is a restricted area,' the commander said, his stern voice filtering through his helmet.

The bystander, a city resident whom Sabine didn't know, crawled back up and scurried off. The stormtrooper commander then gestured. His squad scanned the streets for other trespassers.

Right as the commander turned towards the wall, Sabine climbed over the ledge. She lay flat along the top and waited. One heartbeat. Two heartbeats. Three . . .

She hoped that if one of the stormtroopers did spot her, he would pause in fear at the sight of her Mandalorian helmet. There were few signs of her people in the galaxy these days other than the notorious bounty hunter Boba Fett, who wore Mandalorian armour. His captures and kills had only helped spread the legend that the Mandalorians were the most fearsome warriors in the galaxy.

One day, maybe her own name would have a similar effect. Sabine Wren. Another Mando you didn't want to mess with. A great warrior

STORM
TROOPER

and a great artist.

The sounds of boots echoed again on the pavement and started to fade. The stormtroopers were marching away. Sabine was safe – for the moment.

'Spectre-5 to *Ghost*,' Sabine whispered into her mic.

Hera's voice came over her helmet comlink. 'This is *Ghost*. We are in position and awaiting your diversion.'

'Copy that,' said Sabine. 'This is going to be fun.' Even if Hera and Kanan weren't ready, she was. Like any good Mando, Sabine Wren was always ready.

She pushed herself up to stand atop the wall. 'Very fun.'

On the other side of the wall lay an Imperial airfield packed full of shiny, factory-new TIE fighters so pristine Sabine could almost smell the fresh paint.

The spotlight from a guard tower rotated her way. She stooped and ran along the top of the wall. The spotlight didn't catch her before she leapt down off the wall.

She landed lightly, almost silently, on the tarmac. She took a moment to survey the airfield. She spotted some guards and moved to avoid being noticed.

Sabine sprinted across the tarmac to the nearest TIE fighter. Soon she was hidden in the shadow of one of its wings. The wing would provide a perfect surface on which to accomplish her mission.

She removed her mini airbrush from her belt and shook the attached canister. Then she pressed down on a nozzle and called on her talents.

Sabine began to paint.

CHAPTER 5
Imperial stormtrooper

TK-626 walked with his comrade MB-223 down the line of TIEs. This was their 108th patrol of the airfield that night. And still no sign of rebels. They were too scared to come over the wall. Too scared of stormtroopers like TK-626.

They were right to be scared. The Empire had recruited him straight out of school. His detention record for bullying had supposedly put him at the top of their list. In fact, the

Imperial recruiter had told him that bullies made some of the best stormtroopers. Bullies didn't question orders or think for themselves. They didn't care that they lost their names for numbers. Bullies just wanted to pick on people who were different from them – like rebels.

TK-626 wished there was a rebel to catch in the airfield. Then he could prove his loyalty to the Empire. Yet all he heard was the constant chirp of Lothalian crickbeets. And all he saw was row after row of new TIE fighters. The stormtrooper commander had told them to be careful not to bump or scratch any of the TIEs. TIE pilots could be very protective of their craft and loved to push around lower-ranked stormtroopers.

The crickbeets suddenly stopped chirping. Something shushed like a gust of wind. But there was no wind that night. TK-626 grabbed his comrade's arm. 'You hear that?'

MB-223 yanked his arm free. 'I don't hear –' He looked around. For a second time, there was

TIE FIGHTER

the shushing sound. It came from behind two of the nearest TIEs. 'Wait . . . yeah. What is that?'

TK-626 brought his rifle up to ready. Perhaps they *would* catch a rebel that night. 'This way,' he told his comrade, walking to the two TIEs. The other trooper also readied his weapon and followed.

TK-626 stopped between the fighters.

'What in the –'

On the wing of a fighter glowed the outline of what looked like an enormous purple bird. And the intruder who had painted it was none other than . . . a *girl* in Mandalorian gear?

'What do you think you're doing?' barked MB-223.

The intruder continued airbrushing, not distracted in the slightest. 'What does it look like?' she asked, spraying a wide arc of paint. 'Art.'

TK-626 looked at MB-223. Artists were almost as bad as rebels. They could draw, paint, and create things he couldn't. And for that they deserved to be crushed.

MB-223 levelled his rifle at the intruder. TK-626 did the same.

'W-well, stand down!' shouted MB-223.

'Or we shoot!' yelled TK-626. Basic training had drilled that reaction into him. Shoot first; ask questions later.

The intruder turned her helmet to them.

TK-626 could almost detect a smile under her T-shaped visor. 'OK. Shoot,' she said. 'What are you waiting for?'

That was exactly what he and MB-223 did, without hesitation. Everyone knew not to joke with stormtroopers. It was a crime punishable by death.

But their shots sizzled through the air and hit the TIE behind her instead. She had ducked beneath the cockpit just in time. And now one of the new TIEs had burn marks on the metal. Its pilot would not be pleased.

'You call that shooting?' the intruder yelled out. 'I think you boys need a little more time on the practice range.'

The stormtroopers ran after her, not taking their fingers off the triggers. Yet as the intruder wove between fighters, their shots only pockmarked the airfield and the TIEs.

TK-626 knew they'd be reprimanded for all the damage. But their punishment would be worse if they let this intruder escape. She could

be a rebel.

While MB-223 continued pursuit, TK-626 stopped and pressed his hand to his helmet comlink. 'This is TK-626. There's an intruder on-site.'

Their commander replied immediately over the comm. 'On our way.'

TK-626 rejoined MB-223 near another TIE. The other trooper looked about in disbelief. 'Where did –'

'Over here, bucket-heads!' the intruder said from behind.

MB-223 wheeled around. 'There!' he said, firing away. But the intruder wasn't there, either.

'You guys are too predictable!' she said, behind them again. TK-626 spun and saw her figure swerve between two rows of TIEs. He and MB-223 chased after her, snaking through the TIEs, their blasters on full-fire mode.

This intruder was quick. Their bolts always

seemed a moment too late to hit her. Worse, she laughed at them.

'Missed again!' she said from somewhere near. 'Always by the book! I read your book,' she taunted. 'It's a short one.'

TK-626 didn't like being mocked. It made him furious. Didn't she know what he was? He whirled – and stopped himself at the last second from triggering another round at his commander and three other stormtroopers.

'What have we got?' the commander asked.

'One intruder in Mando gear, still at large,' MB-223 reported.

The commander motioned in each direction. 'Split up. Capture her. I want her alive.'

The six stormtroopers dispersed. TK-626 hoped he'd be the one to catch her. You didn't laugh at Imperial stormtroopers and get away with it.

CHAPTER 6

Sabine stood on the cockpit of the TIE she had painted, watching the stormtroopers spread out to search for her. She jumped down when no one was looking in her direction.

This would be a good opportunity to complete her final mission objective, but she couldn't do that just yet. It wouldn't be right to leave her painting unfinished.

Sabine gave her mini airbrush a shake and added some strokes to the starbird she had sprayed on the TIE's wing. But her painting wasn't quite complete yet. It didn't have her signature touch.

'Something's missing . . .' she said, pulling a circular object off her utility belt and plopping it between the wings she'd painted. 'There, perfect!' Now the starbird had a beak, with a tiny light that blinked. Her signature.

She wished she could admire her work a little longer. But every blink of the beak told her time was running out for her diversion to succeed. She had to gather the troopers together into a group, then sneak back into the city without being noticed.

Sabine raced off, spying white armour behind a nearby TIE. She leapt up to grab a handle on the cockpit-wing attachment and twirled her legs in front of her. One of the stormtroopers approached her. 'Hands up, you rebel scum!' Sabine used her speed and landed a devastating kick to him. The trooper fell, his backside smacking the tarmac. 'Ha! Too slow!'

she said. The trooper rolled and fired, but she was already circling another TIE.

The trooper's frustrated yell brought three more troopers her way. She darted between and underneath the TIEs, laughing as the Imperials fired at her and missed.

The commander summoned all the stormtroopers back to him. Sabine slipped past them and made it to the wall. As she climbed, she could hear their electronically compressed voices.

'Intruder was headed your way!' the commander shouted to the trooper she'd kicked.

'I had her!' the trooper replied.

'Isn't this where we started?' said the one who had identified himself as TK-626 over the comm.

Sabine heaved herself onto the top of the wall, then twisted her body around. She could see the stormtroopers examining the blinking beak. 'Uh-oh,' she heard TK-626 say when the light became steady.

Uh-oh was right. She hadn't come here just to tag machinery. Her art always had a purpose. That day it was to teach those Imperial bullies a lesson.

Sabine dropped off the wall right as the beak on the TIE fighter exploded, destroying the vessel and knocking all the stormtroopers

back to the tarmac.

Her signature was none other than a
paint bomb.

The ground was shaking when she landed.
Alarms rang out in the night. Sabine could
hear the stormtroopers' groans. She wished
she could see their expressions when they

noticed their armour was covered in purple paint.

'That was some diversion, Sabine,' Hera commed from the *Ghost*. 'Did the job so well we can see the explosion from here.'

Sabine reached for the underside of her helmet. 'Forget the explosion,' she said. She pulled her helmet off, wanting an unfiltered view of her minor masterpiece. 'Look at the colour.'

A beautiful purple cloud rose above the airfield. But it wasn't just any cloud. It formed the shape of a starbird, with flashes of gold for eyes. And slowly, the ghostly bird spread its wings across the heavens.

Sabine smiled. Someday soon, she hoped, the oppressive Empire would be brought down, and those thousand thousand worlds would know her name and her art.

She put her Mandalorian helmet back on and walked into the city.

PART 3
ENTANGLEMENT

CHAPTER 7

Garazeb Orrelios entered the alley with his bo-rifle slung over his back. A light wind rustled his gray fur. Rubbish and dust blew back and forth. He had come here to meet his friend and fellow rebel near the marketplace in the lower levels of Lothal's capital city. But as Zeb looked around, there was no sign of Kanan Jarrus anywhere.

His comlink crackled. 'Zeb! Where are you?' said Kanan.

Zeb. Everyone called him by that nickname,

because few species could roll the *r*'s the way you were supposed to in his native Lasat tongue. He missed hearing his language spoken correctly. It was so rare these days. The Empire had done all it could to put his species on the endangered list.

Zeb grabbed his comlink and held it near his sharp-toothed mouth. 'I'm at the rendezvous point. Where are you?'

Kanan's voice sounded irritated over the comlink. 'You're not at the rendezvous point, because *I'm* at the rendezvous point.'

Zeb looked around the alley again, then scratched his chin. This didn't make sense. Maybe he had misheard Kanan's instructions. Humans talked so fast.

'Um, where's the rendezvous point again?' he asked Kanan.

A sigh preceded Kanan's voice. 'In the alley by the marketplace.'

Zeb turned back toward the marketplace. Halfway down the alley, two Imperial

stormtroopers neared a snout-nosed, one-
metre-tall Ugnaught and an astromech droid.
The droid wasn't doing anything associated
with his primary function of navigation. His
repair arm held out a fruit that his master was
selling from a crate.

Zeb frowned. He didn't care much for
street merchants or astromechs. Most street

merchants thought Zeb was a big, gruff oaf and tried to rip him off when they sold him things. And astromechs beeped too much. He couldn't count the number of times he had wanted to shake Chopper when the droid was being a smart mouth.

On the other hand, Zeb cared even less for Imperials. He kept his eyes on the stormtroopers as he spoke to Kanan through his comlink. 'Well, I'm in an alley.'

'And yet clearly not in the *right* alley,' Kanan said.

The troopers jabbed their rifles at the crate, scattering the Ugnaught's merchandise. Clearly they wanted something other than fruit. The squat Ugnaught cowered back in fear.

Zeb scowled, moving his neck to the side, cracking it. 'Yeah, well, there's a lotta alleys in this town,' he responded.

He pushed down on his hard-boned

knuckles, cracking them, too. Then he wiggled his clawed toes and gave them a good crack. He always did this before moving into action. There was no better feeling in the universe. It got his muscles loose.

Bam! One of the troopers kicked the astromech. The little droid fell on its photoreceptor with a clang and a squeal.

Zeb started toward them. That was no way to treat anything – not even an astromech.

'Hagwa je killya, dolpa kikyuna!' said the frightened Ugnaught in Huttese.

'What? Is that a bribe?' the trooper shouted who had kicked the droid. 'Well, now you're under arrest!'

'Noah, noah,' the Ugnaught said. But his protests went unheard. Imperial stormtroopers rarely knew or spoke anything other than Basic, even though Huttese was a common trading language. Zeb understood. He was big and he was gruff, but he wasn't an oaf. All

this Ugnaught had said to the stormtroopers was not to hurt him because he was a loyal, tax-paying citizen.

'I can't believe it! That is an offence!' the trooper said to his comrade. Neither seemed to care about figuring out what the merchant had really said. He looked back at the whimpering Ugnaught. 'Stop whining. We're here to protect you.'

'Yeah.' The other trooper took the Ugnaught's credit box and cleaned out all the coins and credit chips. 'But the Empire's protection can be expensive,' he said, laughing.

His laugh didn't last long. Having advanced on the distracted troopers, Zeb grabbed each with an enormous hand and slammed them into each other like toy soldiers. They both crumpled to the ground.

Zeb's comlink crackled again. 'So are you going to make the rendezvous or not?' Kanan asked.

Zeb grinned down at the little Ugnaught, who seemed even more scared. At first he thought it was because of his size, but then he saw four more stormtroopers rushing into the alley.

'Hey! You! *Stop!*' the lead trooper yelled, raising his blaster.

'It's possible I may be a little late,' Zeb said into the comlink. He began to run in the other direction before the stormtroopers could open fire.

'You're *already* late,' Kanan said.

If Zeb didn't find somewhere to hide soon, he might be more than late. He might never show up to whatever alley Kanan wanted to meet in.

CHAPTER 8

Zeb rushed onto a security landing pad in an alley near the marketplace. 'Zeb, what's going on?' Kanan shrilled over static.

The pilot on the landing pad looked up from a maintenance check of his grounded TIE fighter. 'What's going on?' he yelled at Zeb. 'This is a restricted area!'

'Right, so I'm *definitely* going to be late,' Zeb said into his comm.

'Lat*er*,' said Kanan. 'Lat*er*!'

Zeb didn't have time to argue with Kanan.

He only had time to make a fist and smash it against the pilot's helmet. The pilot keeled over just as the troopers rushed into the alleyway and opened fire. Zeb ducked behind the TIE fighter for cover and clambered up to the top of the cockpit. He jumped out of the alley and kept running, losing the troopers. He angled into another alley and found safety behind a wall.

He watched the stormtroopers rush past him. Then he reached out and grabbed the last stormtrooper in the group.

Given the similarities in their size and strength, Zeb could identify with Wookiees. He felt compassion for those brawny tree-dwellers of Kashyyyk, since the Empire had enslaved their species just like they had the Lasat. But he didn't think any comparison did his own species justice. Because he knew *he* was stronger than any Wookiee.

Zeb picked up the trooper and tossed him

IMPERIAL FORCE

into his comrades. In the collision, a trooper's blaster discharged with a loud *ping*.

'Wait, are you fighting stormtroopers?' Kanan asked on the comlink. One of the troopers recovered and raised his weapon at Zeb.

'What makes you say that?' Zeb asked. In one smooth swing, he pulled the bo-rifle off his back and knocked the trooper's gun upward. A bolt shot into the air.

'I heard blaster fire . . .' Kanan said.

Zeb activated the stun function on his weapon. His rifle converted to its other form: a bo-staff. Energy danced from the tip down its length.

Zeb jabbed the staff at the trooper. The man yelled, shocked off his feet.

'And screaming!' Kanan added.

Zeb rotated his weapon to wield it like a club. 'There may be more screaming.'

And there was. He bashed two stormtroopers, who both fell back in a heap of moans.

'Oh, that's great,' Kanan remarked on the comlink. 'You got lost in the middle of a mission and decided to start your own battle – again!'

'Didn't decide,' Zeb said, beating down the fourth trooper. 'It just happened this time.'

Behind Zeb, the TIE pilot teetered up from the ground. He did his best to aim his pistol at the brawny Lasat and tapped his comm. 'LS-607 needs reinforcements.'

'How many intruders?' responded the commander over the Imperial frequency.

'How many?' the pilot repeated, somewhat confused, still swaying from Zeb's punch. His finger quivered on the trigger.

Though Zeb didn't have eyes in the back of his head like some species, his auditory senses were exceptional. He overheard the pilot's exchange behind him.

Zeb slung his bo-staff over his shoulder and turned to the pilot, pretending to count on his paw. If the pilot couldn't see how many intruders there were, Zeb would make it clear. He closed his fingers against his palm until a single finger remained.

IMPERIAL FORCE TROOPERS

'One,' Zeb said, pointing the finger at himself.

The pilot kept his blaster trained on Zeb. 'Commander, just get over here!' he said into his comm.

'Copy that!' the commander said.

With reinforcements coming, the time for fun and games was over. Zeb leapt towards the TIE fighter. The pilot fired.

Zeb grabbed on to the wing rod of the TIE fighter and spun around it like he was a juvenile Lasat on a tree branch. All the pilot's blasts missed. The pilot stepped closer for a better shot. Zeb kicked, gaining speed as he revolved around the rod.

The pilot fired again. But Zeb no longer held the rod. He had launched himself into the air – and landed on the pilot's shoulders.

The pilot yelped, yanked off the ground by Zeb's toes, while Zeb reached out for a landing strut. He swung around the strut like a monkey-lizard, released his toe grip, and flung the pilot away. The man hit the pad with a thud. This time he didn't get up.

Zeb did another spin around the strut to vault himself atop the TIE fighter. A familiar voice buzzed him on his comlink. 'Zeb, are you embarrassing the Imperials again?'

'Honestly, Kanan, it's not hard to do,' Zeb said.

He looked down with a grin at the eight stormtroopers coming from the nearby alley. Two of the troopers had dents in their helmets. These must be the ones he'd bashed together after they harassed the Ugnaught fruit seller. Zeb's grin widened.

The stormtrooper commander looked up at the TIE where Zeb stood. 'Weapons to "stun". Bring him down,' he ordered.

The troopers switch-clicked their weapons and fired. Zeb catapulted off the TIE high into the air. Blaster bolts flew to the clouds while Zeb crashed down right in the middle of the squad. He kicked, grabbed, and punched, tossing stormtroopers around like they were snowflakes.

'Can't get a clear shot!' said a trooper.

Zeb knew that in a close fight like this, blasters were hard to aim, because shots might

BRUISER ZEB

hit comrades. So he kept smashing the troopers together, making them as close as could be.

'I mean, do they even bother training these bucket-heads?' Zeb said, wanting both the troopers and Kanan on his comlink to hear. 'My old gran's a better fighter, and she's only two metres tall!'

The commander stepped away from the brawl. He lifted his blaster and aimed carefully. Zeb didn't see him shoot. But he sure felt it.

The shot had hit Zeb in the chest, sizzling his fur. Electricity coursed through Zeb's nerves. The other troopers held their positions, watching the giant Lasat sway.

Zeb gritted his teeth. He thought of his old gran. She'd lived for 300 dust seasons on Lasan, through much worse troubles than this. He was going to do the same.

He was only hit by a stun bolt, after all.

Zeb slowly turned towards the commander, his expression of pain returning to a grin. 'That . . . stung.' He pulled his bo-staff free from his back.

'Weapons on "kill"!' said the commander.

It became a race between Zeb shifting his staff into rifle mode and the commander changing the energy setting of his blaster.

And it was a race the commander lost.

'Weapons on –' the commander repeated, cut off when the energy blast from Zeb's rifle knocked him back.

Four of the troopers, however, got their weapon settings changed. At once, they fired at Zeb.

The Lasat dived under the TIE fighter and rolled under the pod-shaped fuselage that contained the cockpit. Blasts ricocheted off the metal. Zeb got up on one knee just as a bolt scorched a lower panel on the TIE. Liquid fuel began to drip out.

'Well, that's not good,' Zeb said.

'What's not good?' Kanan enquired over their link.

Zeb scrambled to his feet and ran as fast as his long legs would carry him. The troopers continued to fire. None hit the Lasat, yet many of their blasts ignited the liquid fuel.

Seconds later, the TIE fighter blew apart into a million pieces, sending the stormtroopers flying across the landing pad.

Yes, Zeb thought, *there's nothing like embarrassing Imperials.*

CHAPTER 9

The Ugnaught fruit seller and his rusty astromech neared from the mouth of the alley. Flames shimmered out on the landing pad. Stormtroopers groaned, trying to push themselves up.

Zeb suddenly blocked the view, striding into the alley with his bo-rifle over his shoulder. He brushed off all the black soot that covered his fur.

As Zeb moved towards the Ugnaught and the astromech, the Ugnaught ran to his crate of goods and grabbed his credit box. He rattled it, offering what little was left in it to Zeb. The astromech droid tweedled.

Zeb ignored the credit box. Instead, he picked up a round, juicy fruit and held it up to the Ugnaught. The Ugnaught's snout puckered, but then he bowed, saying, *'Dobrah gusha tu trawbbio grandio, mendeeya.'*

In Huttese his words meant something like 'It would be an honour if the great one took it.' Zeb thought it was probably the first time a street merchant called one of his species 'great' rather than 'oaf'. But Zeb was too hungry to reply. The fruit looked delicious. He brought it to his mouth for a bite.

'Zeb! I see smoke,' Kanan commed over the link. 'Was that a TIE fighter exploding?'

Kanan seemed to know when to press Zeb's buttons. Instead of tasting a sweet morsel of fruit, Zeb coughed out a tiny black cloud. He'd breathed in the wretched stuff from the

explosion. But he couldn't let Kanan know.

'No.' Zeb coughed again, unable to hold it back. Kanan would hear it and get angry if Zeb didn't tell the truth. 'OK, yes.'

There was silence over the comlink. Kanan was probably mad. Kanan usually got upset when embarrassing Imperials wasn't part of the plan.

'Nice,' Kanan said.

Kanan's approval caught Zeb by surprise. Maybe the human was turning over a new leaf. 'I thought so,' Zeb replied after taking a big bite of the fruit. He knew it was rude to talk with his mouth full. But he couldn't help it, not with Kanan actually complimenting him.

'OK, stay put,' Kanan said. 'I'll follow the smoke and pick you up.'

The droid's dome suddenly swivelled. The Ugnaught ducked behind his crate. Another squad of stormtroopers charged into the alley.

'I'll be here,' Zeb said. He took another bite, then tossed the fruit over his shoulder and unslung his bo-rifle. He hoped Kanan would be late. He had more Imperials he needed to embarrass.

PART 4
PROPERTY OF
EZRA BRIDGER

CHAPTER **10**

Ezra Bridger adjusted the straps of his backpack and walked over the rise. The plains before him stretched out to the horizon. There was no marker of civilisation except a rust-coloured communications tower in the distance. Everything else was just grass, a calm and endless stretch of it, stroked by a gentle wind and warmed by the golden light of the late-afternoon sun.

Ezra descended the hill into the plains. He was fourteen. Most looked at him and saw a boy. A *kid*. Sometimes they even called him that horrible name: urchin. But he didn't think of himself as any of those. Not after all he'd been through. Kids had parents. Kids had apartments or houses. Kids had dinner served on plates while sitting at tables.

Kids didn't live on the city streets, like Ezra.

On the streets, you grew up fast. You had to if you wanted to eat and protect yourself from scavengers, Imperials, and other villains. You learnt how to survive.

But outside the city was different. Here there was no noise. Here there was just the sun and the wind and the grass and the night sky full of stars. Here, on the rolling prairies of Lothal, there was peace.

Here Ezra could be just a kid.

He felt a sudden tingle, a nudge. He could never pinpoint where it came from, whether his head, heart, or chest. Those who knew him thought he had lightning-fast reflexes. But it was more than a reflex. It was like an

EZRA

instinct. And it always came without warning – or more appropriately, it *was* a warning . . . that something was about to happen. Something serious.

Ezra looked around. He didn't feel in danger. There weren't any predators this close to the city. But he trusted this instinct. It had

saved his skin too many times for him not to.

Then there was a screaming across the sky – the sound of engines being pushed to their limits. Ezra looked up to see a diamond-shaped cargo freighter, pursued by a flat-winged TIE fighter, fly overhead. The TIE closed in and fired its cannons.

The lasers shot past, as the cargo ship had started a loop. Within a few heartbeats, it was behind the TIE, adding cannon fire of its own.

These shots hit.

The freighter passed over Ezra and rocketed off into the clouds while the smoking TIE corkscrewed downwards. It barely cleared a hill before making a fiery crash. The ground shook.

That little feeling nudged Ezra again. Not to hide, but to seek. Somehow, in some way, he was connected to this crash. Maybe he could even find something of value in the wreckage.

Ezra held on to his backpack straps and ran towards the rising smoke.

CHAPTER 11

Ezra crested the hill,

breathing hard. Down below burned what remained of the TIE fighter. Bits and pieces lay strewn all over the charred grass. Smoke coiled out from its cracked cockpit.

Ezra scanned the land around him. He didn't see signs that anyone else had noticed the crash. Grass rustled as it always did for miles in every direction.

He looked back at the crashed TIE. His lips curved into a crooked grin. He'd never had an opportunity like this. The TIE's military-grade hardware could fetch a huge price on the black market.

Ezra hurried down the hillside towards the crash site. Soon he was climbing the TIE's broken support and swinging towards the cracked canopy. He hadn't seen any movement

inside the cockpit, but he had to make sure.
If the pilot was still alive and needed help, he
might be able to get a reward.

'Mister!' he shouted.

A form shifted in the cockpit, then groaned.
Ezra climbed closer for a better look inside.
'Hey, you OK? You alive?'

The form shifted again, turning a black
helmet toward Ezra. The pilot, it seemed, was
very much alive. 'Get your hands off my craft!
This fighter is the property of the Empire!'
he yelled.

'Guess that's a yes,' Ezra said to himself.
He backed off a step to breathe. More smoke
came out of the cockpit – so much that the pilot
began to cough. His helmet must have been
damaged if it couldn't filter out all the fumes.

The pilot hit the emergency switch to
open the canopy. It popped up a few inches,
then jammed.

Ezra grabbed a free edge of the cockpit,
watchful for jagged shards of transparisteel,

then swung himself up behind the canopy hatch. He hated helping Imperials, especially ungrateful ones. But if he didn't get the canopy open, the man would suffocate. And then Ezra would never get a reward.

Ezra wiggled his fingers under the canopy hatch and began to yank it upwards with all his strength.

'I told you to get off this ship!' the pilot said, struggling between coughs.

'Not much of a ship anymore.' Ezra pulled and pulled, his backpack bouncing behind him. The hatch was really stuck. 'Besides, I'm just trying to open her up –'

Ezra nearly lost his balance as the canopy snapped open. Dense clouds of smoke puffed out. Ezra let out a deep breath. That had been hard work.

Free from the smoke, the pilot removed his helmet. His coughs settled as he breathed fresher air. He stared up at Ezra. Without his TIE helmet, the man seemed like any ordinary

FREEDOM FIGHTER
EZRA

guy, not a brainwashed Imperial. He seemed
like a person who might actually be grateful for
having his life saved.

The man's face hardened. His eyes pinched
into mean dots. He was not appreciative in the
slightest.

Ezra met the man's stare. He could play

this game, too. 'Hey, don't say "thank you" or anything.'

'Thank you?' The pilot bristled, insulted. He looked like he wanted to spit at Ezra. 'Please. I'm an officer of the Imperial Navy. I didn't need your help.'

Ezra tilted his head, looked at the man again, and smiled. 'Course not.'

The pilot huffed and began to rise out of his seat. 'Wait!' Ezra said. He bent down and pushed a hand on the man's shoulder. 'Your sleeve's caught on the flight recorder.'

'It is?' asked the pilot. He couldn't move, the confines were so cramped.

'Let me unhook it for you.' Ezra reached past the pilot with his other hand. Some of the technology here could buy him a month's worth of food.

A panel hinge squeaked as he wrenched it free. 'What was that?' the pilot asked, attempting to look around.

Hands behind his back, Ezra stuffed the

TIE FIGHTER SQUADRON

gadget into his pack. He had no idea what he had got – and he didn't want the pilot to know, either. He continued the conversation as if nothing had happened. 'Why were you chasing that cargo ship? Were they smugglers?'

'That's confidential information,' the pilot said, again attempting to rise. Ezra pushed him back down.

'Whoa, there, sir. Bit of metal caught on your, um, posterior,' Ezra said, indicating the man's backside. 'Wouldn't want an "officer" of the Imperial Navy to split his pants.'

The pilot shook his head, flustered. 'No, I –'

'That just wouldn't be dignified. Hold still, now.' Ezra leaned into the cockpit again, reaching for the other side. 'Almost got it,' he said, rotating an interior bolt near the man's waist.

'There!'

Ezra stood tall, darting his hands behind his back and shoving a second high-tech gadget into his pack. 'Now, remember, sir,' he said, stepping back. 'No thank-yous.'

The pilot fumbled with his helmet as he climbed out of the cockpit. 'Here, I'll take that,' Ezra whispered, snatching the helmet. He didn't have a TIE pilot's helmet in his collection. It would look nice on display inside the tower.

Ezra raised his voice, continuing where he'd left off. 'Because, like you mentioned, you didn't need my help. And besides . . .' He planted a hand on the man's bare head, using it to vault into the air. 'I didn't come to help.'

'Why, you little . . .' The pilot spun, but he was too late. Ezra somersaulted down and landed on the ground, running, with the pilot's helmet tucked under an arm.

'Just came to score a little tech for the black market, you Loth-rat!' Ezra yelled back to the pilot. These gadgets were going to buy him a soft bed and a fancy dinner. *Many* fancy dinners.

CHAPTER 12

Ezra had made it halfway up the hill when he felt that tingle again. Actually, it was more than a tingle. It was like his spine was being rattled. He had to move or he would die.

Ezra followed his instinct and flipped to the left. A cannon blast pounded the hillside where he'd just stood. Unfortunately, he'd dropped the helmet. It tumbled down the hill, skipping over rocks.

Ezra couldn't go back for it now. Incessant

blasts came from the TIE fighter. Ezra rolled, making himself a difficult target to hit. He could almost hear the pilot's voice: *Lucky kid.*

The man was wrong. This wasn't luck. And while Ezra was technically a kid, he played harder than any other kid he knew.

When he came up to his knee, Ezra was holding his most valuable possession – the *other* thing that had saved his life countless times.

His slingshot.

Ezra pulled back on his slingshot's energy stream. A bright, sizzling stunball formed in the pocket field. The TIE laser cannons fired again.

Nudged by his special instinct, Ezra leapt high over those blasts. And still in the air, he quickly slung two stunballs in rapid-fire fashion.

The stunballs were perfectly aimed. They hit the TIE's viewport – then fizzled out.

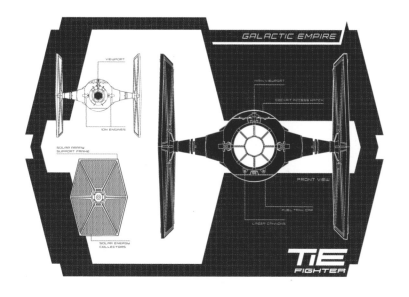

Shocked, Ezra lost focus. His landing didn't go as planned. He fell back onto his backside.

Ezra knew he probably lay in the dead centre of the TIE's targeting scope. A sitting hawk-bat if there ever was one. He could see the pilot looking out at him through the broken canopy. Fingers on the cannon trigger, the pilot allowed himself a cocky grin.

Ezra used that moment to shoot a stunball.

The energy globe arced high – too high to do any damage to the cockpit. Instead, it nicked the edge of the canopy, causing the globe to ricochet – into the back of the pilot's head.

The man crumpled in the seat, dazed. His fingers fell from the trigger, and his face slammed the cockpit dash. He never knew what had stunned him.

Ezra rose, dusting his clothes off. 'Well, that was fun.' He took a breath and looked around. 'Now, where . . .'

He found the TIE fighter pilot's helmet leaning against a rock. He picked it up and examined it. Then he put the helmet on his fist and shook it back and forth like a puppet's head. 'This helmet is the property of Ezra Bridger,' he said, mimicking the Imperial's stern voice.

Ezra stared into the dark lenses that were supposed to shade the pilot's eyes. 'Or it is now, anyway,' he said, and put the helmet on.

The helmet bounced on Ezra's head, many sizes too big. He could hardly see out of those dark lenses. He could hardly breathe.

Discomforts like that had never stopped him before. Ezra came out there to have fun – to be a kid and that was what he'd do.

He held the helmet in place with a hand

and turned towards the outline of the TIE fighter. With his other hand, he saluted. 'Sir! Thank you, sir!'

Then he walked away, skipping over blast craters and weaving around smouldering wreckage. Only when he had reached the summit of the hill did he pause and look back. Smoke plumed up from the crash site like phantom snakes.

Ezra tightened the straps of his backpack and turned around to descend the hill, whistling merrily. The distant communications tower might be a lonely, rusted hulk, but it was his home away from the streets. There he would have fun. There he would enjoy the last rays of the sun and look up at the dawning stars.

There he would find peace.

ABOUT THE AUTHOR

MICHAEL KOGGE has written in the *Star Wars* galaxy for a long, long time. His other recent work includes *Empire of the Wolf*, an epic comic series featuring werewolves in ancient Rome, published by Alterna Comics. He lives online at www.michaelkogge.com, while his real home is located in Los Angeles.